3

# TEEN TITANS GO!®

Raintree

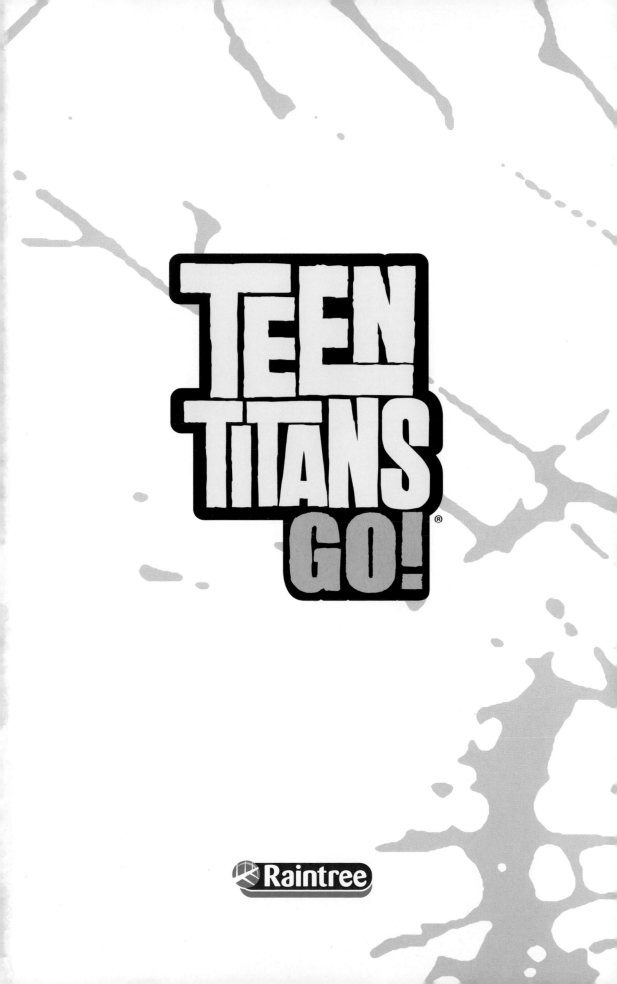

Raintree is an imprint of Capstone Global Library Limited, a company incorporated in England and Wales having its registered office at 7 Pilgrim Street, London, EC4V 6LB - Registered company number: 6695582

www.raintreepublishers.co.uk
myorders@raintreepublishers.co.uk

First published by Raintree in 2014


Ashley C. Andersen Zantop *Publisher*
Michael Dahl *Editorial Director*
Sean Tulien *Editor*
Heather Kindseth *Creative Director*
Alison Thiele *Designer*
Kathy McColley *Production Specialist*

DC COMICS
Kristy Quinn *Original U.S. Editor*

ISBN 978 1 406 27947 4
Printed in China by Nordica.
1013/CA21301918
17 16 15 14 13
10 9 8 7 6 5 4 3 2 1

A full catalogue record for this book is available from the British Library.

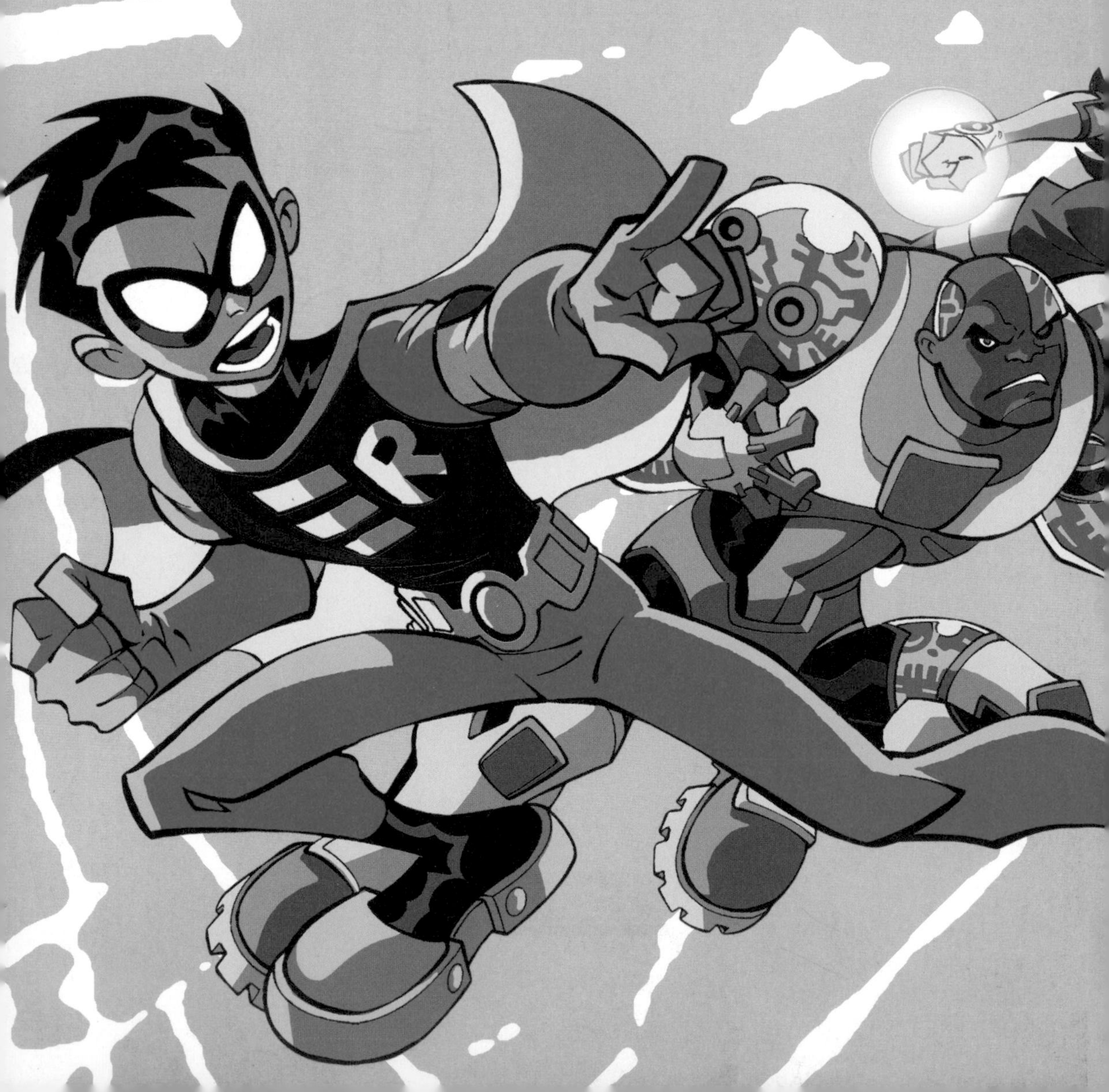

# TEEN TITANS GO!®

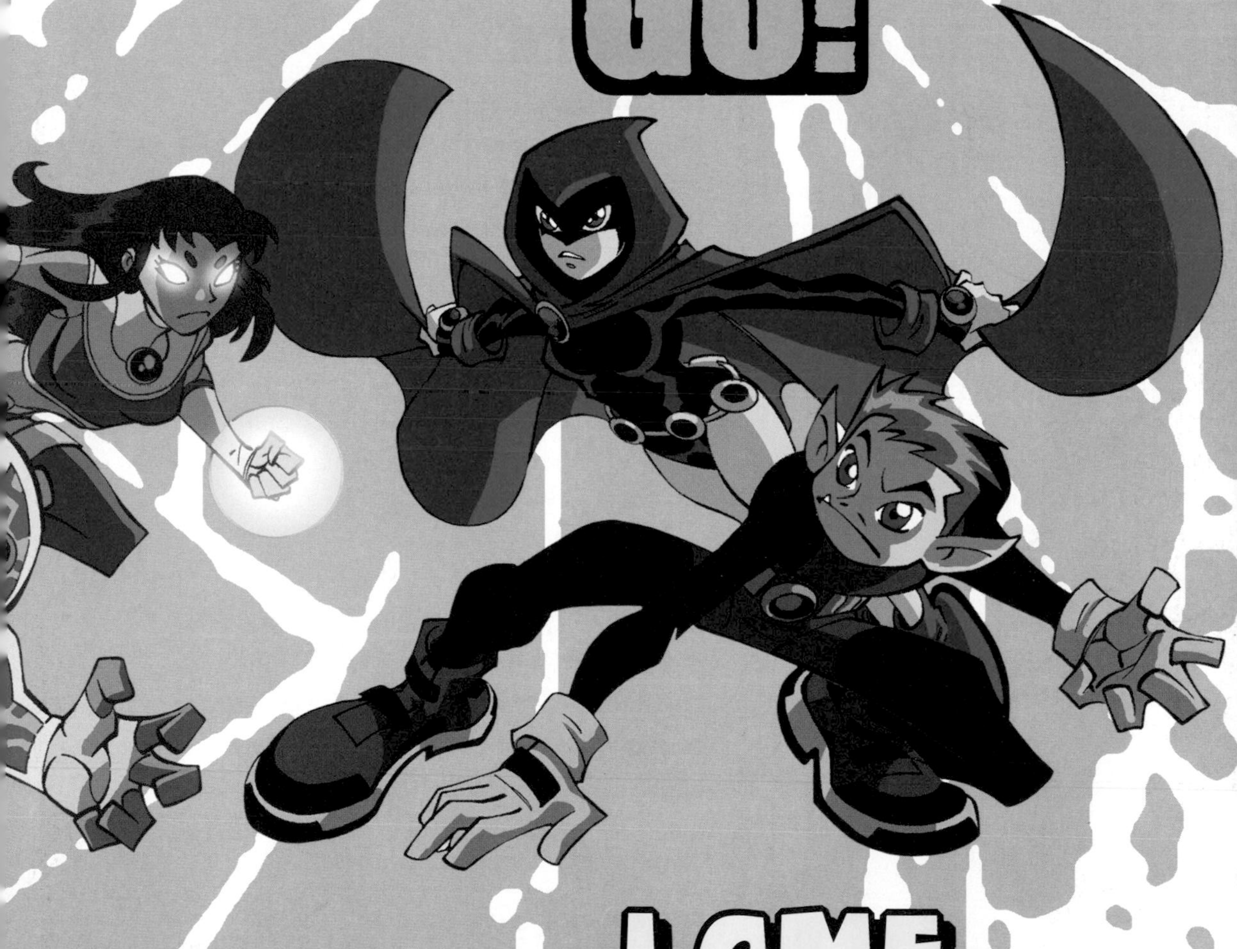

## LAME

J. Torres........................................................ writer
Tim Smith 3 & Lary Stucker........................artists
Brad Anderson........................................ colourist
Jared K. Fletcher...................................... letterer

# TEEN TITANS GO!

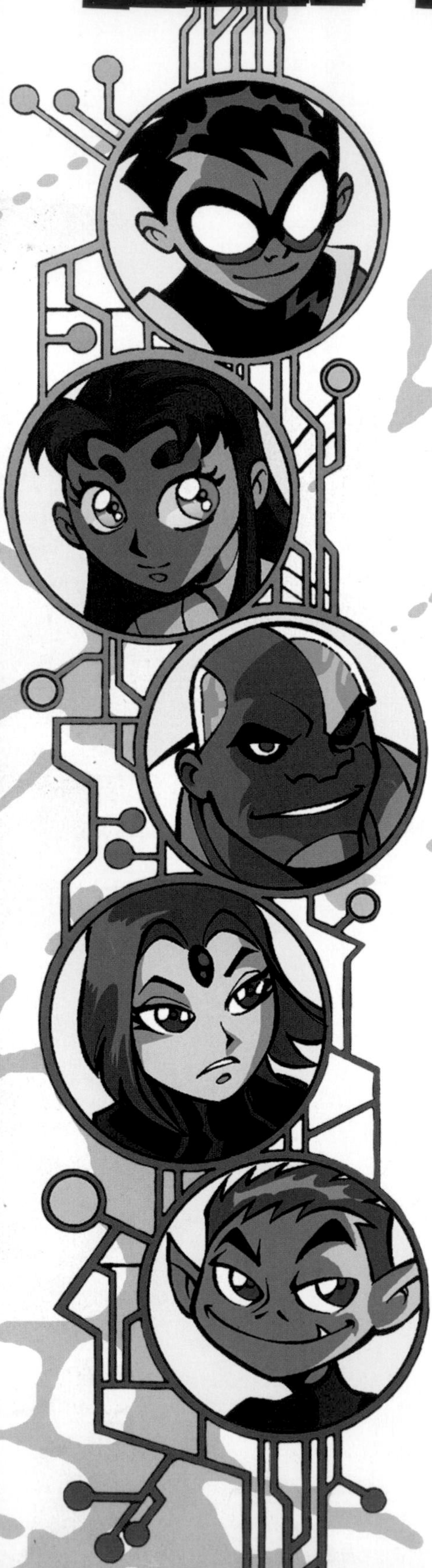

## ROBIN

**REAL NAME:** Dick Grayson

**BIO:** The perfectionist leader of the group has one main complaint about his teammates: the other Titans just won't do what he says. As the partner of Batman, Robin is a talented acrobat, martial artist, and hacker.

## STARFIRE

**REAL NAME:** Princess Koriand'r

**BIO:** Formerly a warrior Princess of the now-destroyed planet Tamaran, Starfire found a new home on Earth, and a new family in the Teen Titans.

## CYBORG

**REAL NAME:** Victor Stone

**BIO:** Cyborg is a laid-back half teen, half robot who's more interested in eating pizza and playing video games than fighting crime.

## RAVEN

**REAL NAME:** Raven

**BIO:** Raven is an Azarathian empath who can teleport and control her "soul-self," which can fight physically as well as act as Raven's eyes and ears away from her body.

## BEAST BOY

**REAL NAME:** Garfield Logan

**BIO:** Beast Boy is Cyborg's best bud. He's a slightly dim but lovable loafer who can transform into all sorts of animals [when he's not too busy eating burritos and watching TV]. He's also a vegetarian.

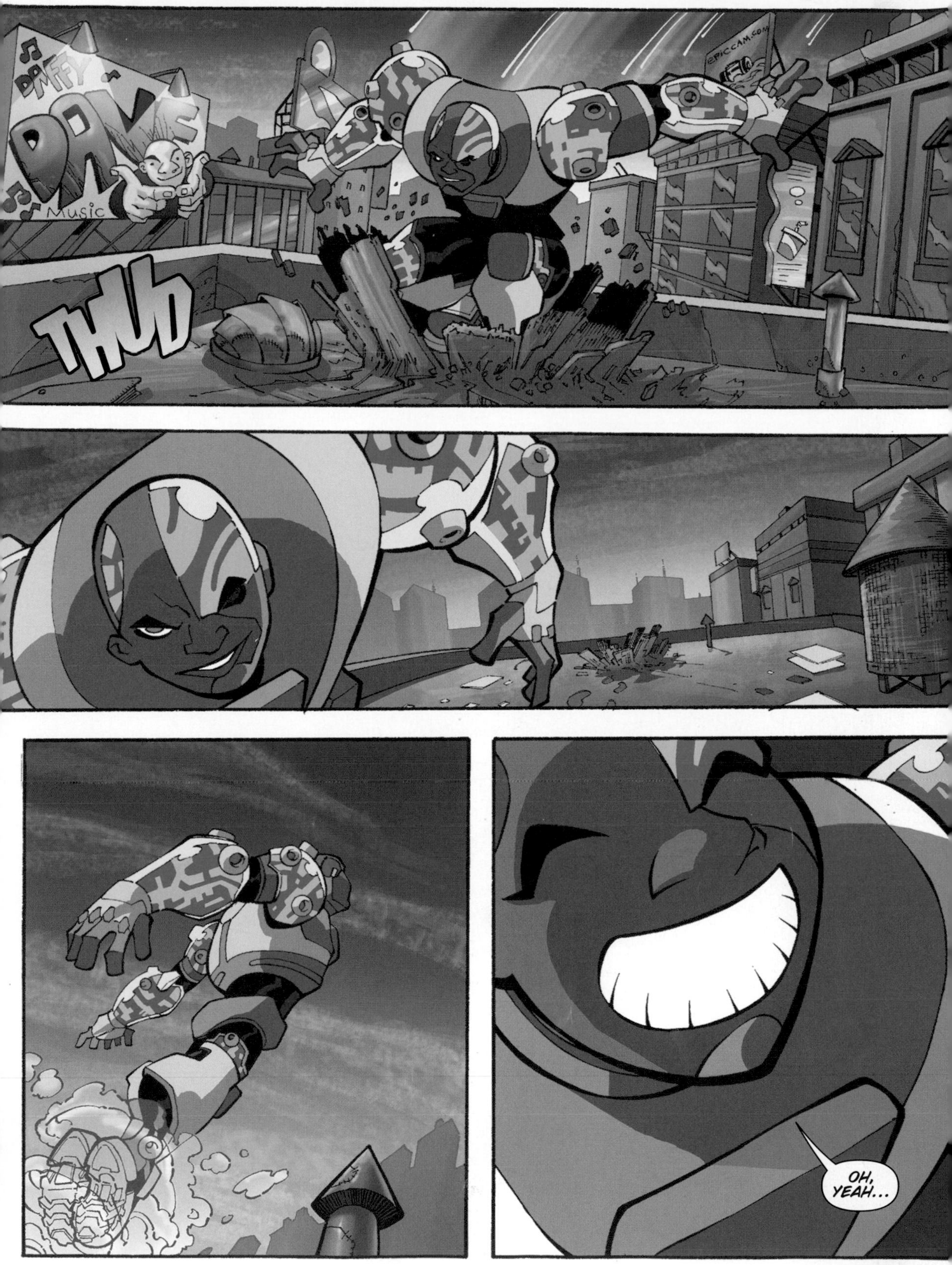
THUD
OH, YEAH...

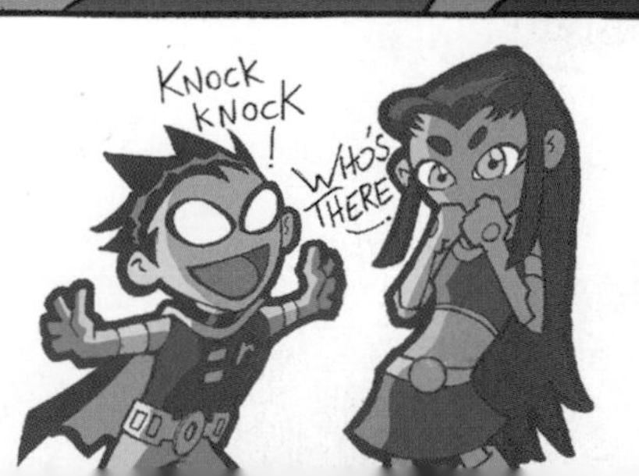
KNOCK KNOCK!
WHO'S THERE

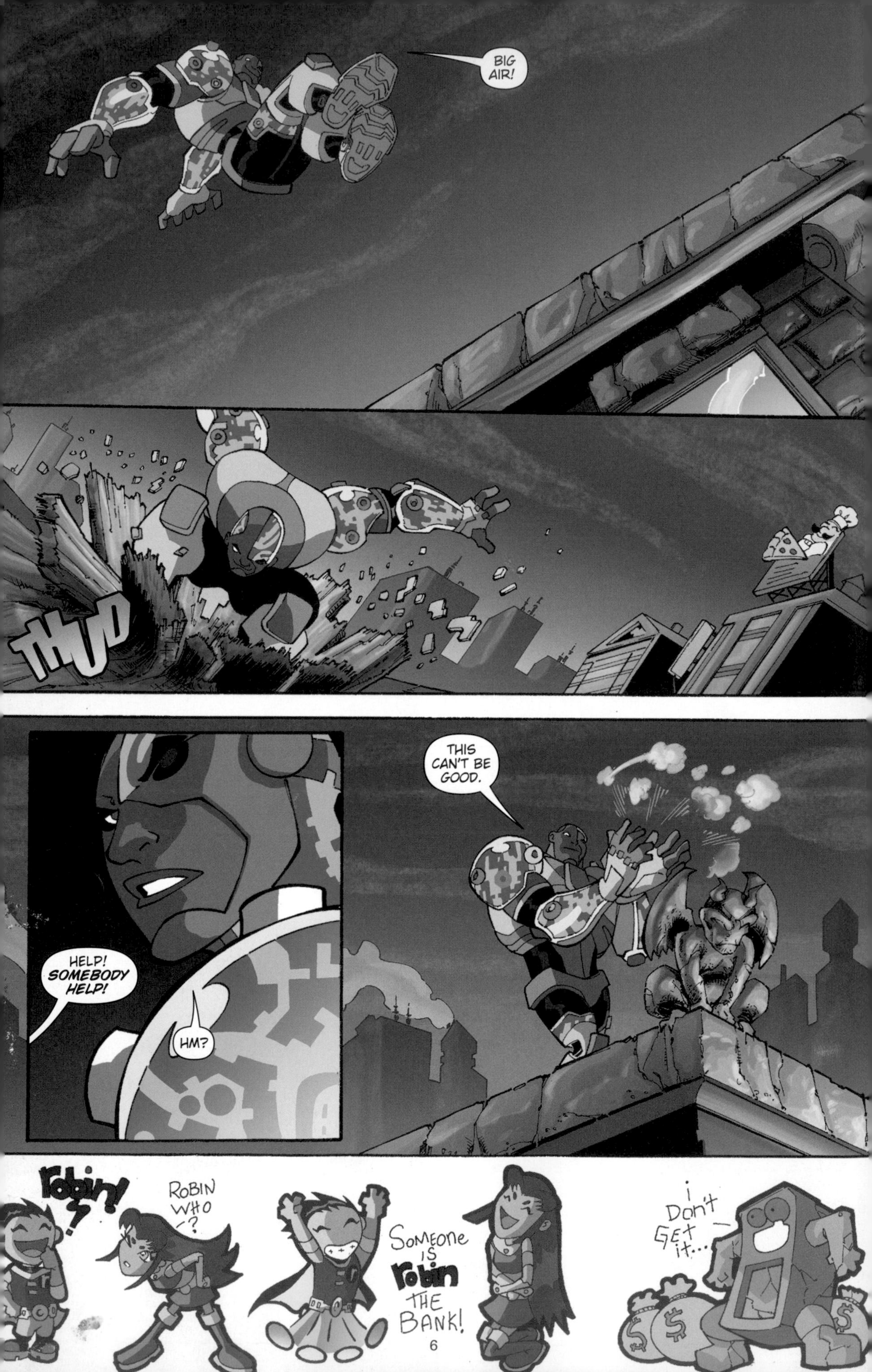
BIG AIR!
THUD
THIS CAN'T BE GOOD.
HELP! SOMEBODY HELP!
HM?
robin!
ROBIN WHO -?
SOMEONE IS robin THE BANK!
I DON'T GET IT...

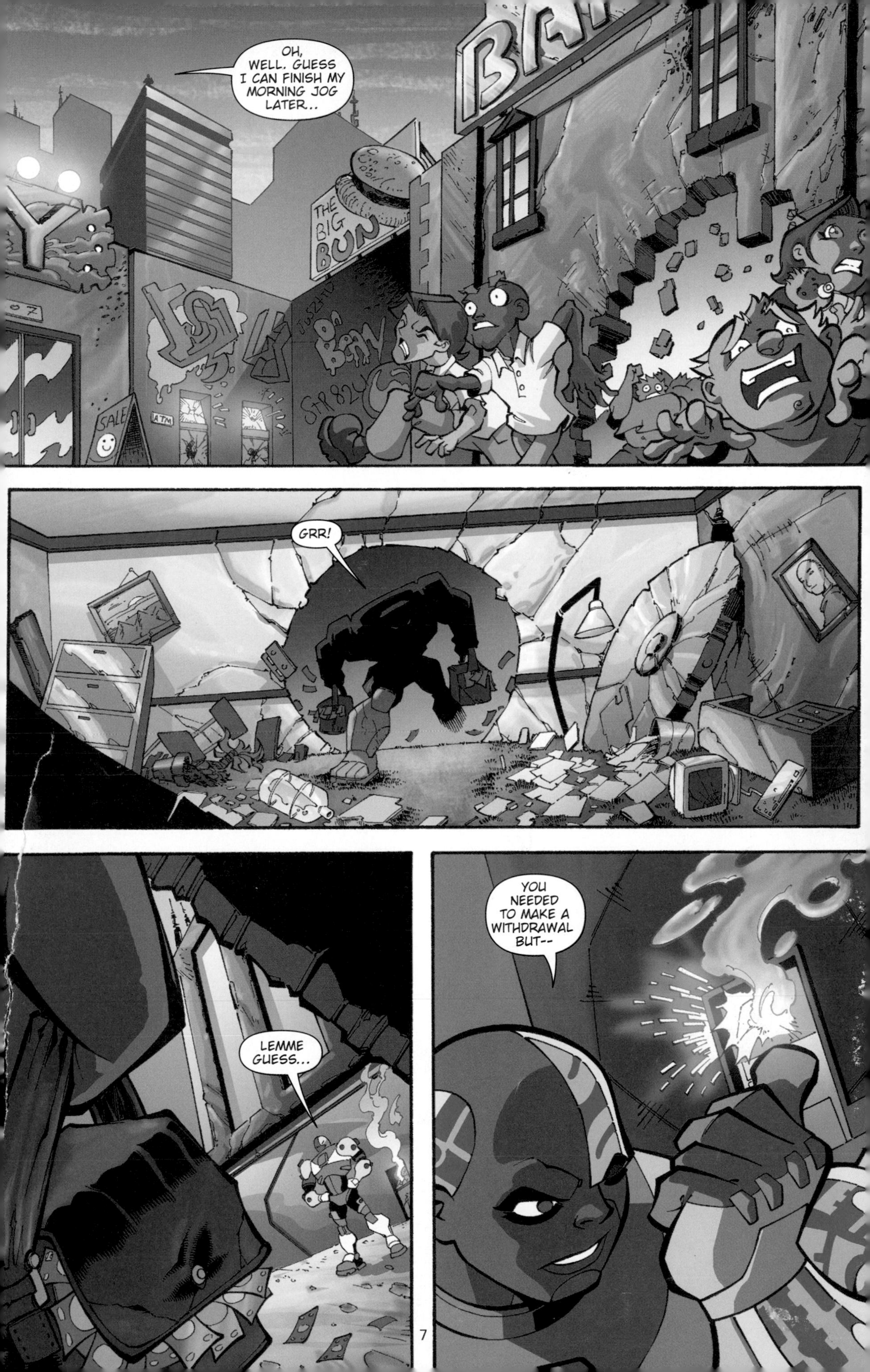
OH, WELL. GUESS I CAN FINISH MY MORNING JOG LATER...
THE BIG BUN
SALE
ATM
GRR!
LEMME GUESS...
YOU NEEDED TO MAKE A WITHDRAWAL BUT--

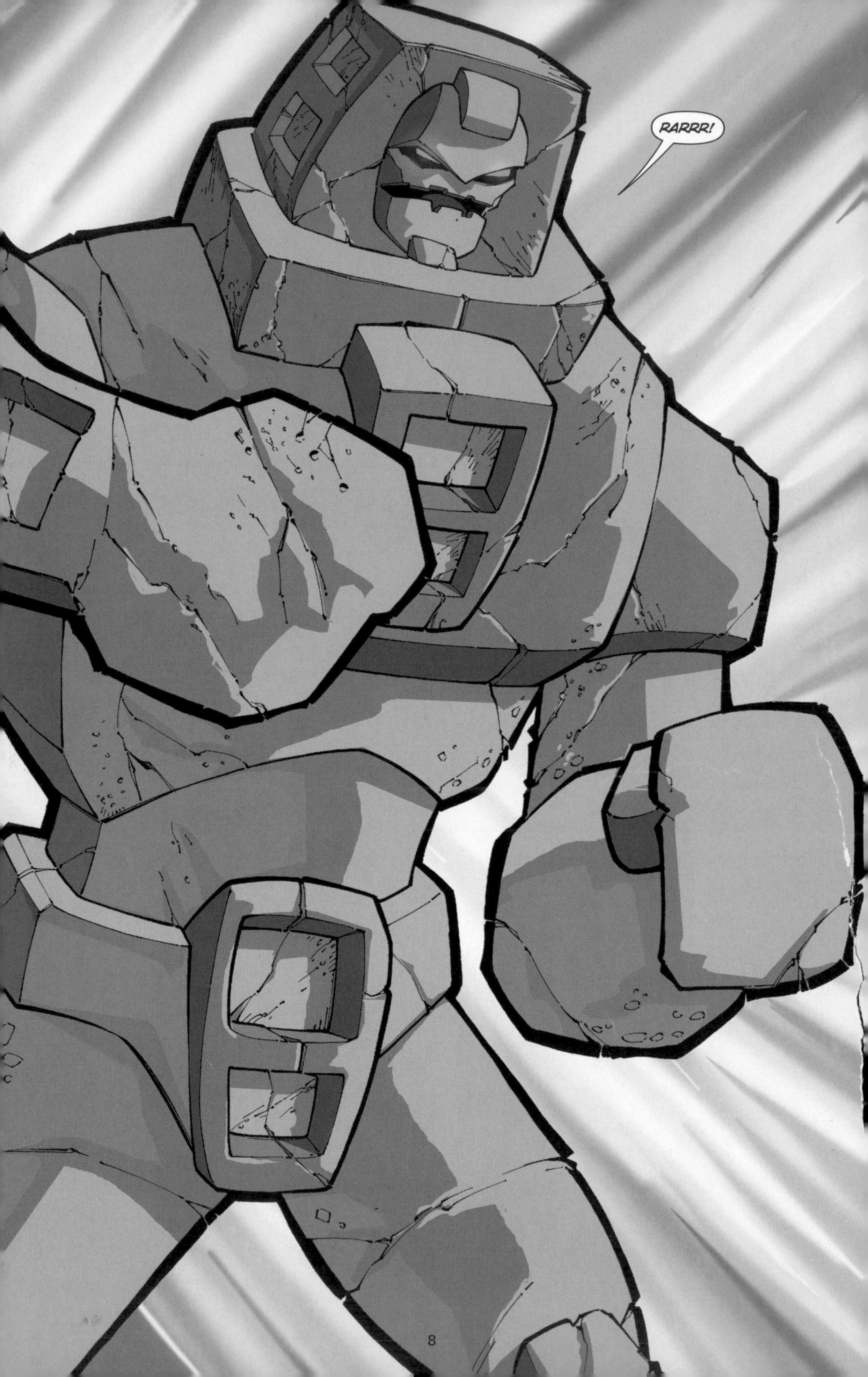
RARRR!

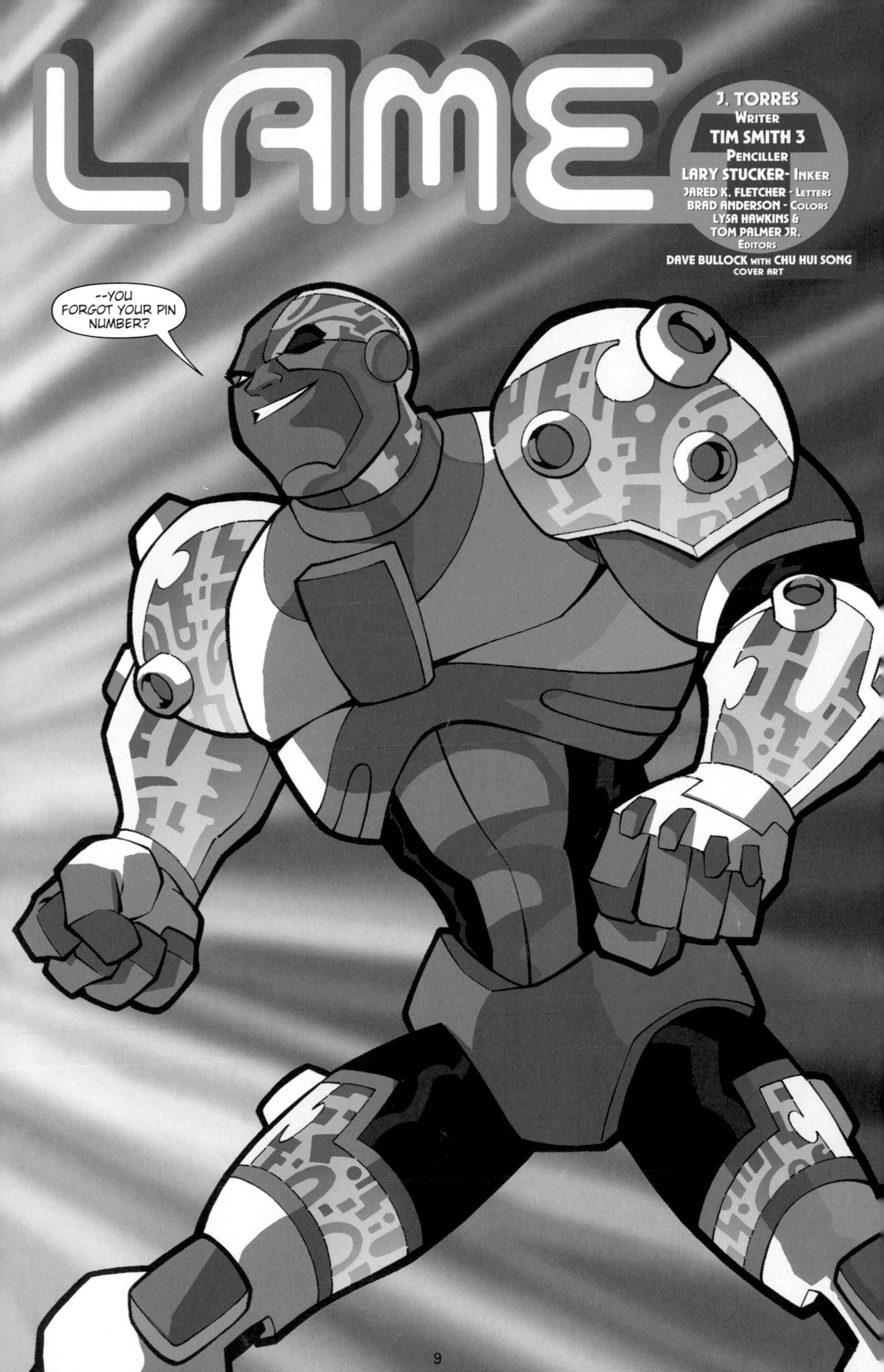
LAME
J. TORRES
WRITER
TIM SMITH 3
PENCILLER
LARY STUCKER- INKER
JARED K. FLETCHER - LETTERS
BRAD ANDERSON - COLORS
LYSA HAWKINS &
TOM PALMER JR.
EDITORS
DAVE BULLOCK WITH CHU HUI SONG
COVER ART
--YOU FORGOT YOUR PIN NUMBER?

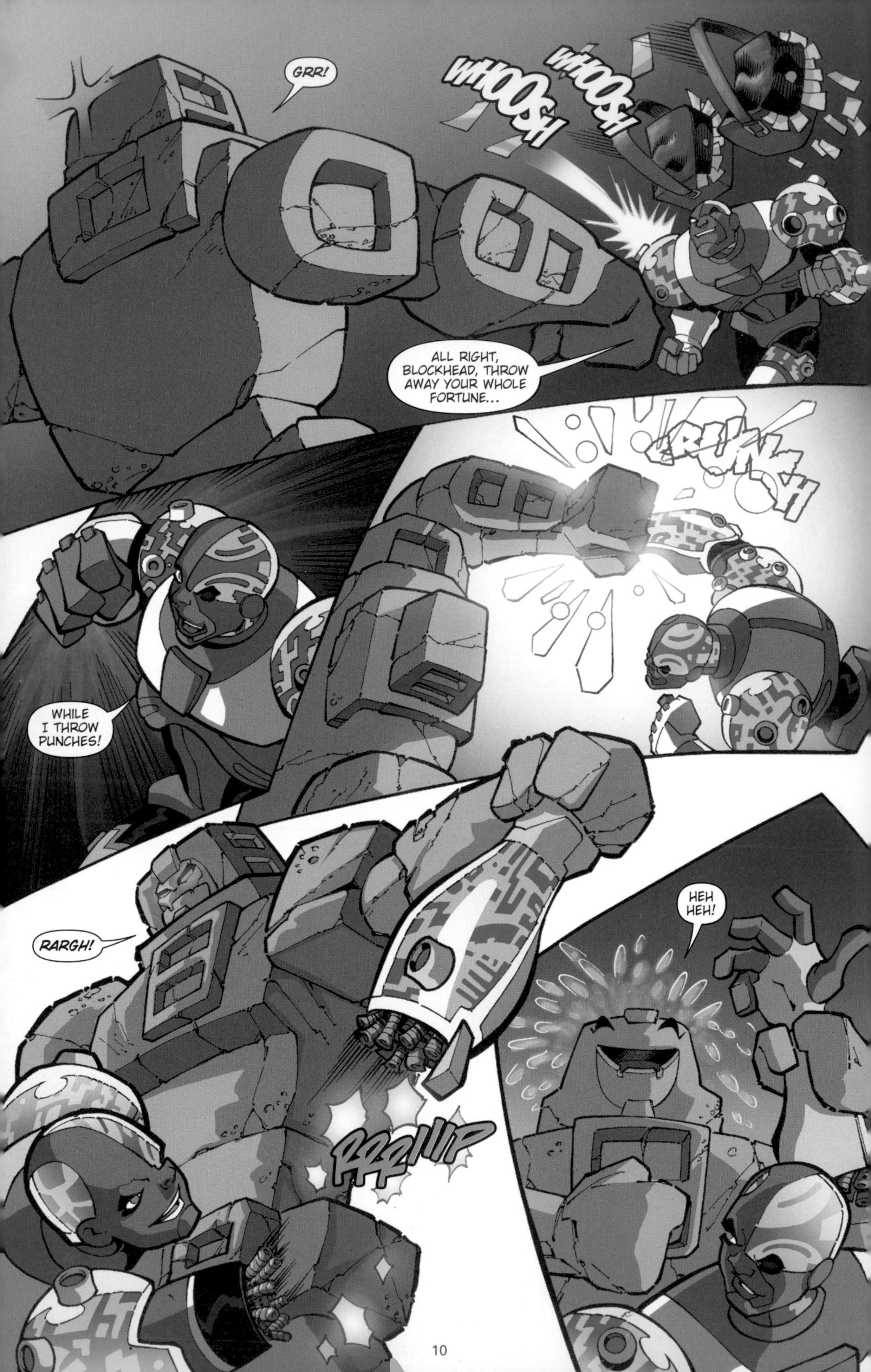
GRR!
WHOOSH
WHOOSH
ALL RIGHT, BLOCKHEAD, THROW AWAY YOUR WHOLE FORTUNE...
WHILE I THROW PUNCHES!
CRUNCH
RARGH!
RRRIIIP
HEH HEH!

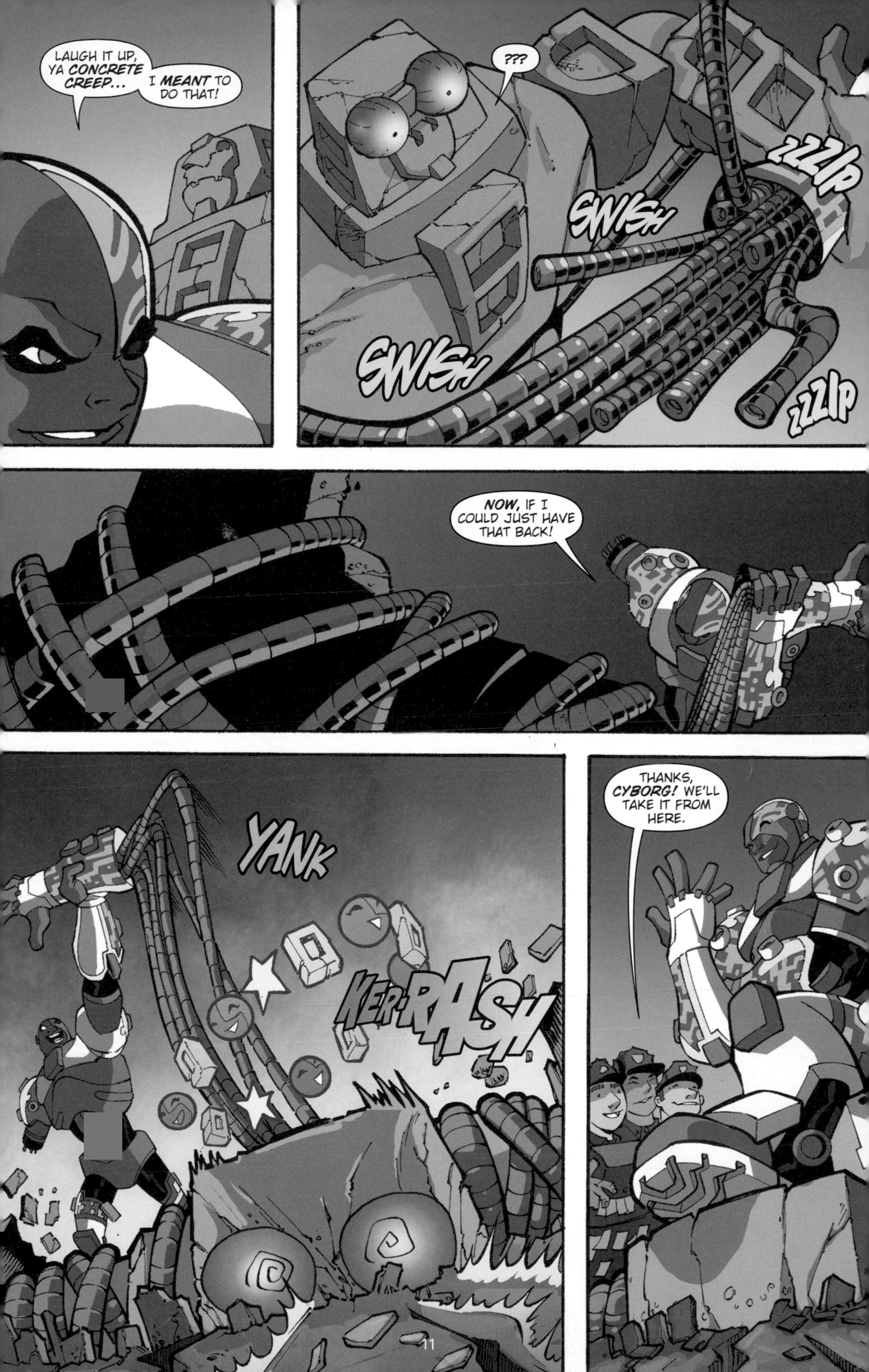
LAUGH IT UP, YA CONCRETE CREEP...
I MEANT TO DO THAT!
???
SWISH
ZZZIP
SWISH
ZZZIP
NOW, IF I COULD JUST HAVE THAT BACK!
YANK
KER-RASH
THANKS, CYBORG! WE'LL TAKE IT FROM HERE.

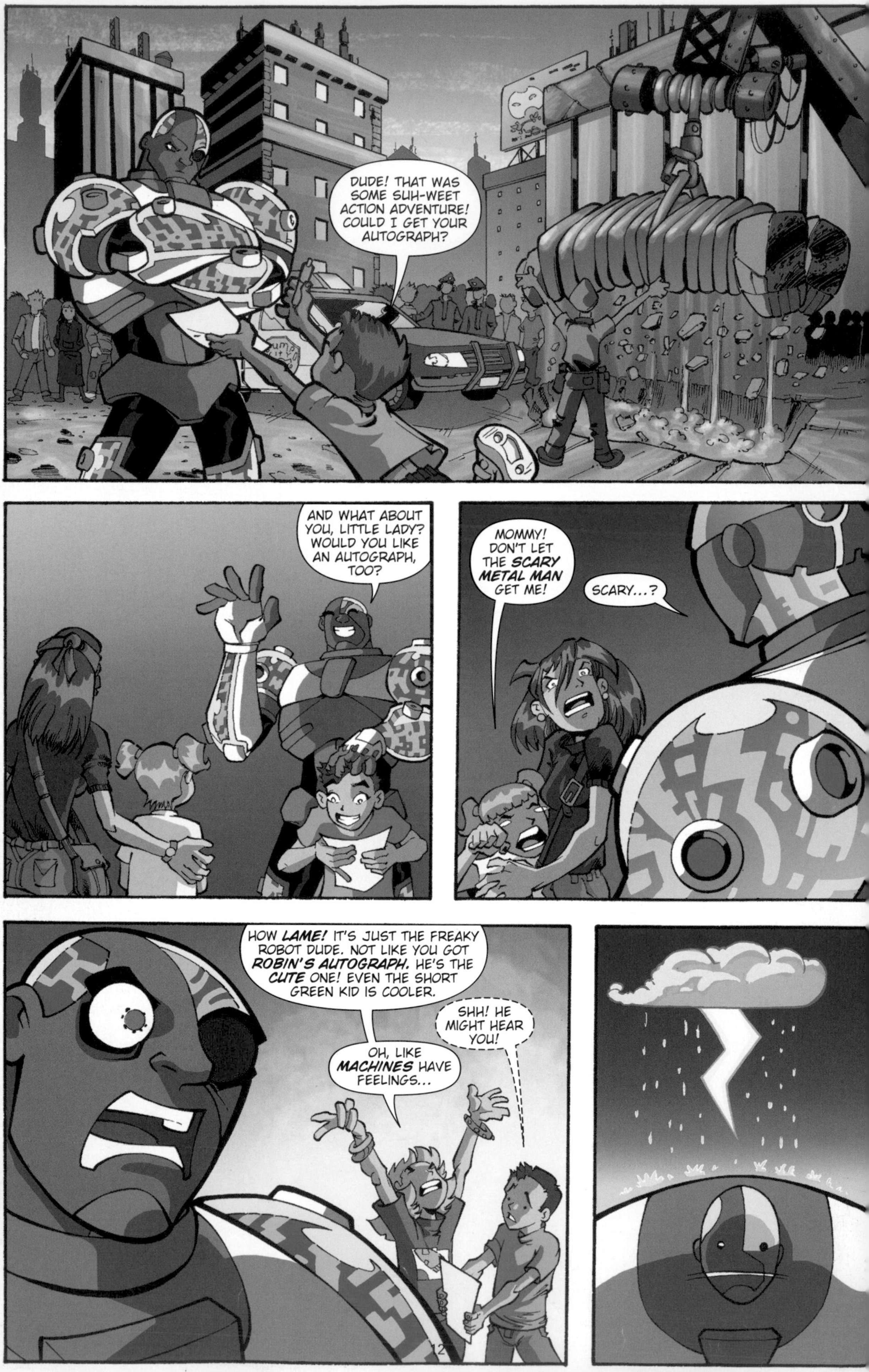

DUDE! THAT WAS SOME SUH-WEET ACTION ADVENTURE! COULD I GET YOUR AUTOGRAPH?
AND WHAT ABOUT YOU, LITTLE LADY? WOULD YOU LIKE AN AUTOGRAPH, TOO?
MOMMY! DON'T LET THE SCARY METAL MAN GET ME!
SCARY...?
HOW LAME! IT'S JUST THE FREAKY ROBOT DUDE. NOT LIKE YOU GOT ROBIN'S AUTOGRAPH. HE'S THE CUTE ONE! EVEN THE SHORT GREEN KID IS COOLER.
SHH! HE MIGHT HEAR YOU!
OH, LIKE MACHINES HAVE FEELINGS...

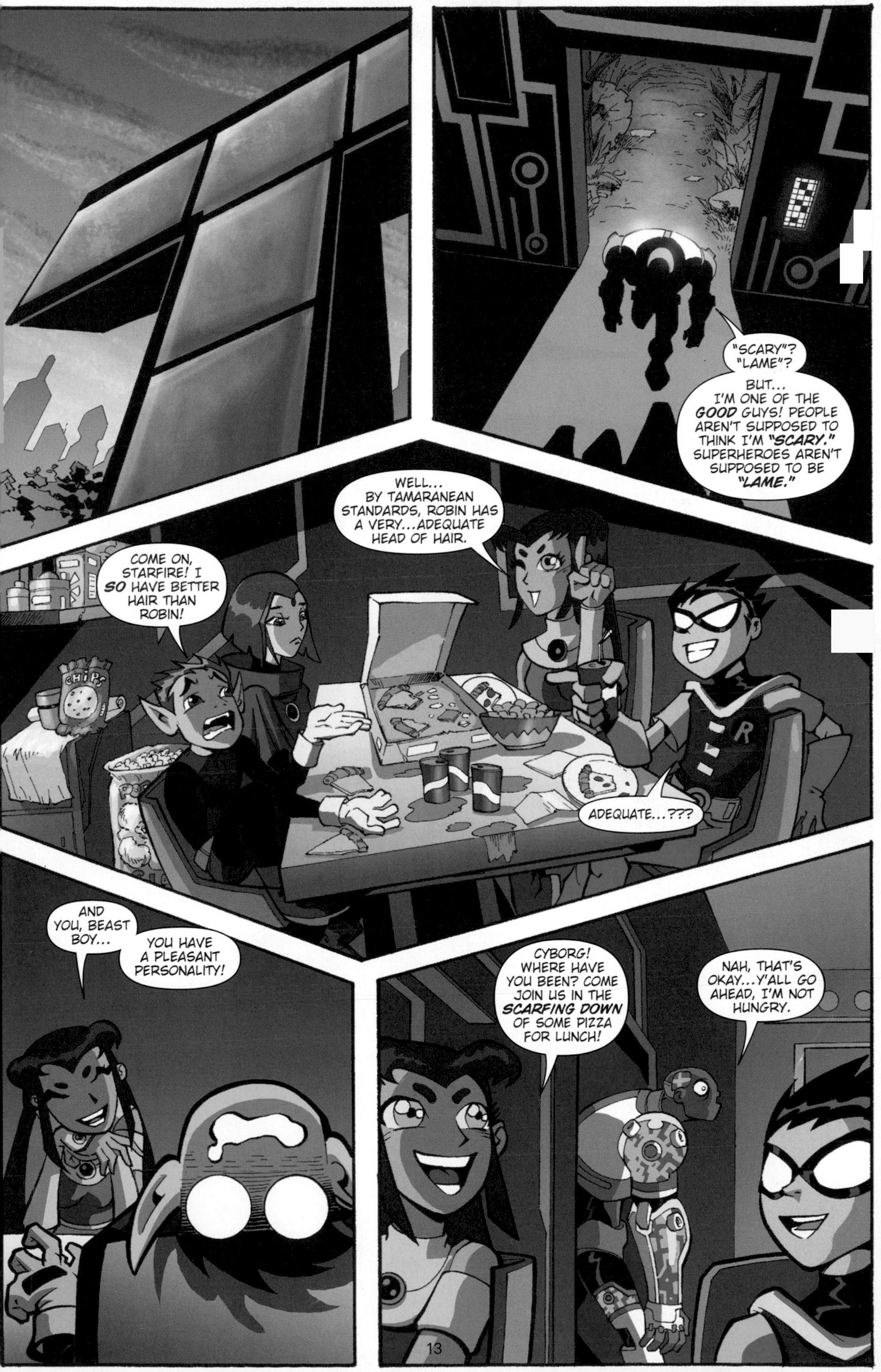
"SCARY"? "LAME"?
BUT... I'M ONE OF THE GOOD GUYS! PEOPLE AREN'T SUPPOSED TO THINK I'M "SCARY." SUPERHEROES AREN'T SUPPOSED TO BE "LAME."
COME ON, STARFIRE! I SO HAVE BETTER HAIR THAN ROBIN!
WELL... BY TAMARANEAN STANDARDS, ROBIN HAS A VERY...ADEQUATE HEAD OF HAIR.
CHIPS
ADEQUATE...???
AND YOU, BEAST BOY...
YOU HAVE A PLEASANT PERSONALITY!
CYBORG! WHERE HAVE YOU BEEN? COME JOIN US IN THE SCARFING DOWN OF SOME PIZZA FOR LUNCH!
NAH, THAT'S OKAY...Y'ALL GO AHEAD, I'M NOT HUNGRY.

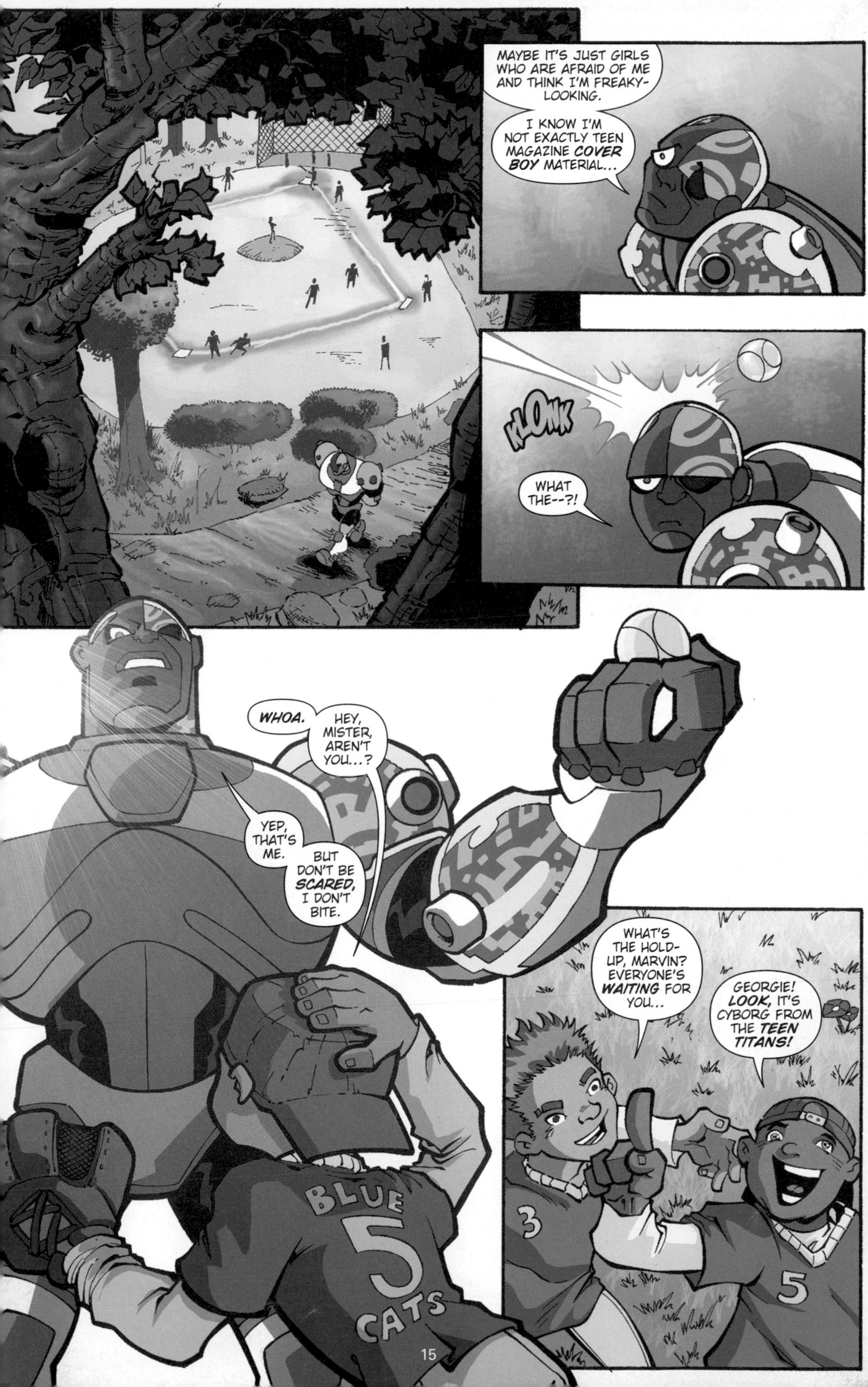
MAYBE IT'S JUST GIRLS WHO ARE AFRAID OF ME AND THINK I'M FREAKY-LOOKING.
I KNOW I'M NOT EXACTLY TEEN MAGAZINE **COVER BOY** MATERIAL...
KLONK
WHAT THE--?!
**WHOA.**
HEY, MISTER, AREN'T YOU...?
YEP, THAT'S ME.
BUT DON'T BE **SCARED,** I DON'T BITE.
WHAT'S THE HOLD-UP, MARVIN? EVERYONE'S **WAITING** FOR YOU...
GEORGIE! **LOOK,** IT'S CYBORG FROM THE **TEEN TITANS!**
BLUE 5 CATS
3
5

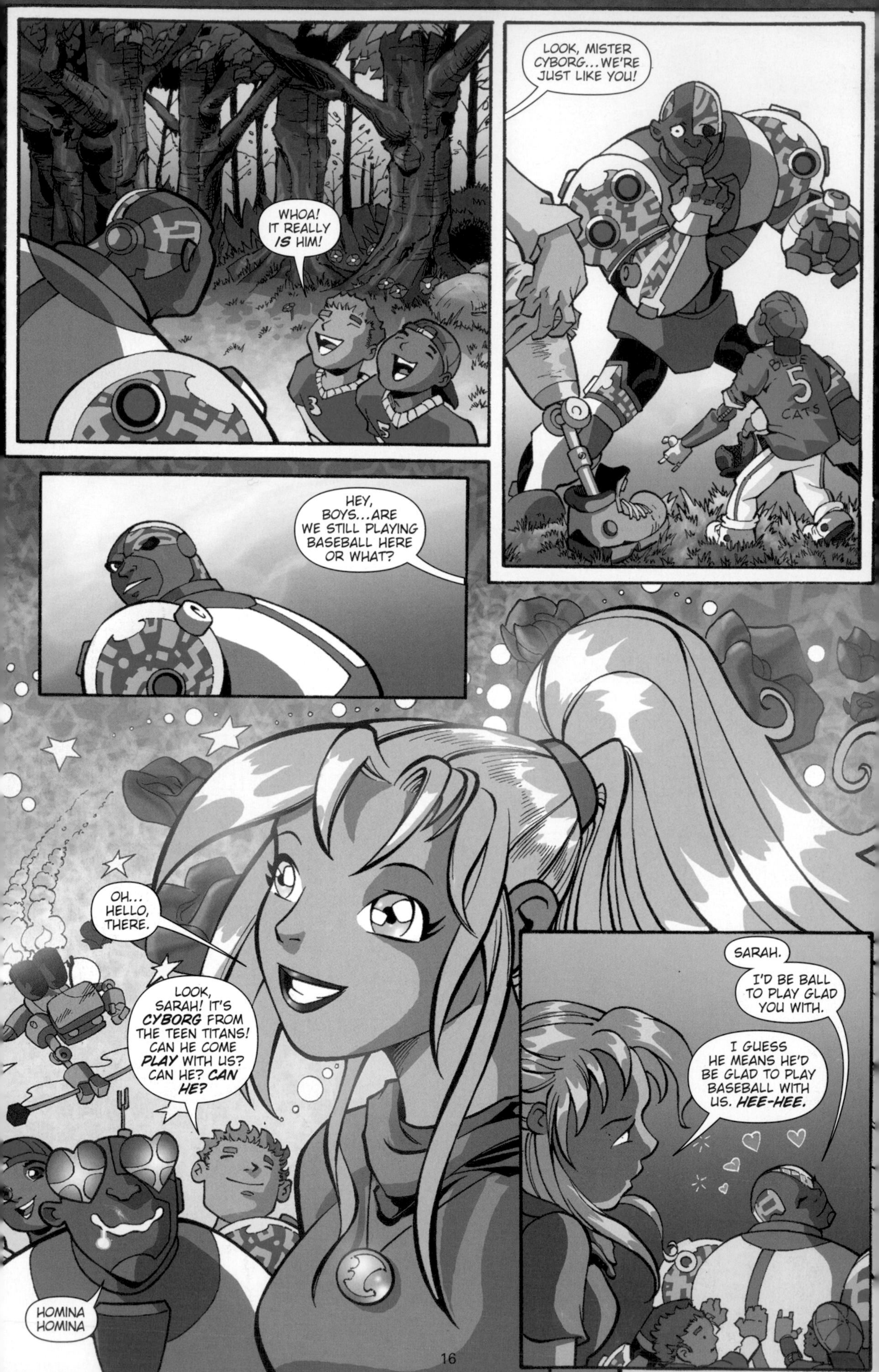
WHOA! IT REALLY *IS* HIM!
LOOK, MISTER CYBORG...WE'RE JUST LIKE YOU!
BLUE 5 CATS
HEY, BOYS...ARE WE STILL PLAYING BASEBALL HERE OR WHAT?
OH... HELLO, THERE.
LOOK, SARAH! IT'S *CYBORG* FROM THE TEEN TITANS! CAN HE COME *PLAY* WITH US? CAN HE? *CAN HE?*
HOMINA HOMINA
SARAH.
I'D BE BALL TO PLAY GLAD YOU WITH.
I GUESS HE MEANS HE'D BE GLAD TO PLAY BASEBALL WITH US. *HEE-HEE.*

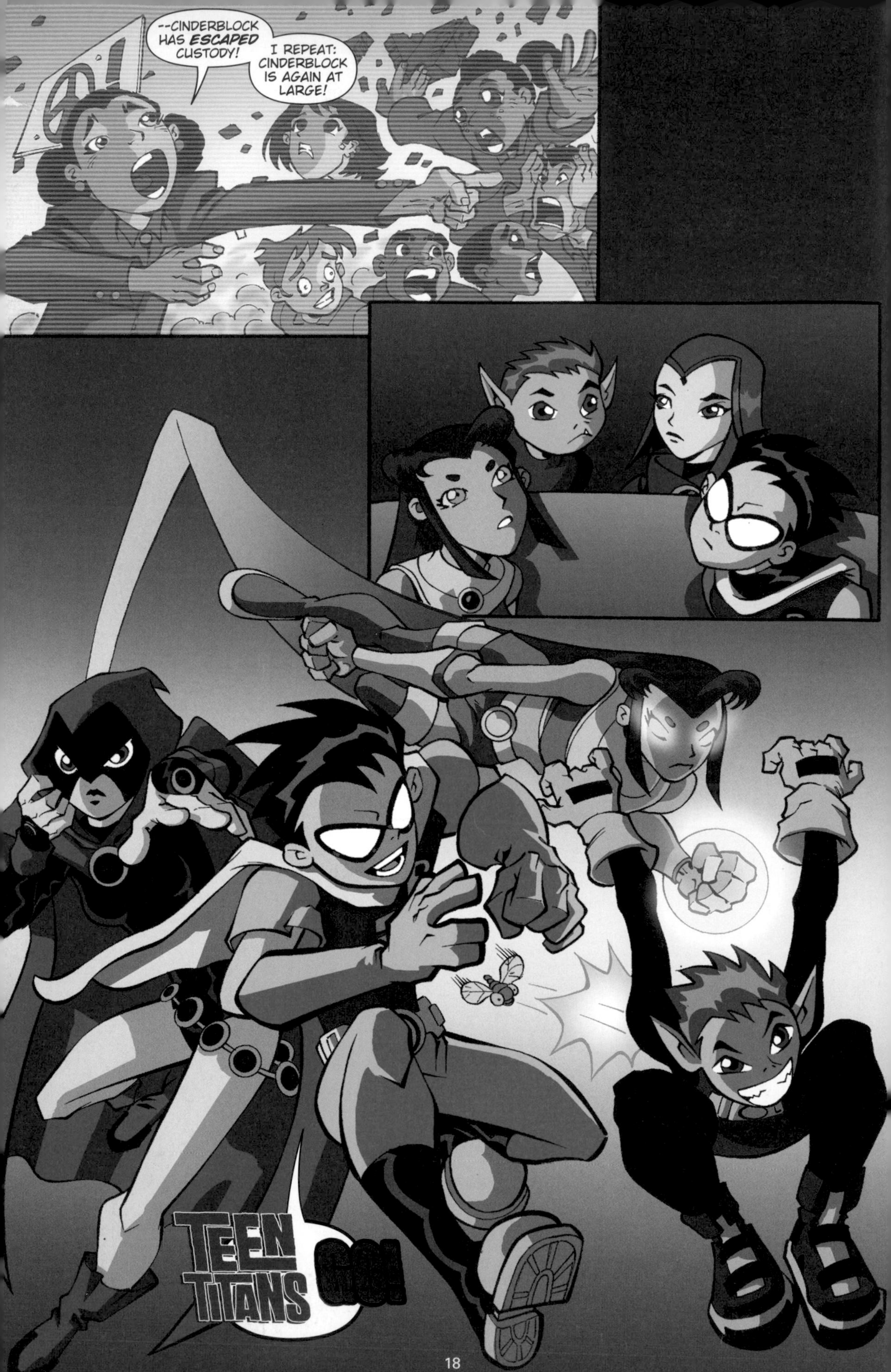
--CINDERBLOCK HAS ESCAPED CUSTODY!
I REPEAT: CINDERBLOCK IS AGAIN AT LARGE!
TEEN TITANS GO!

They are good at catching **Flies!**

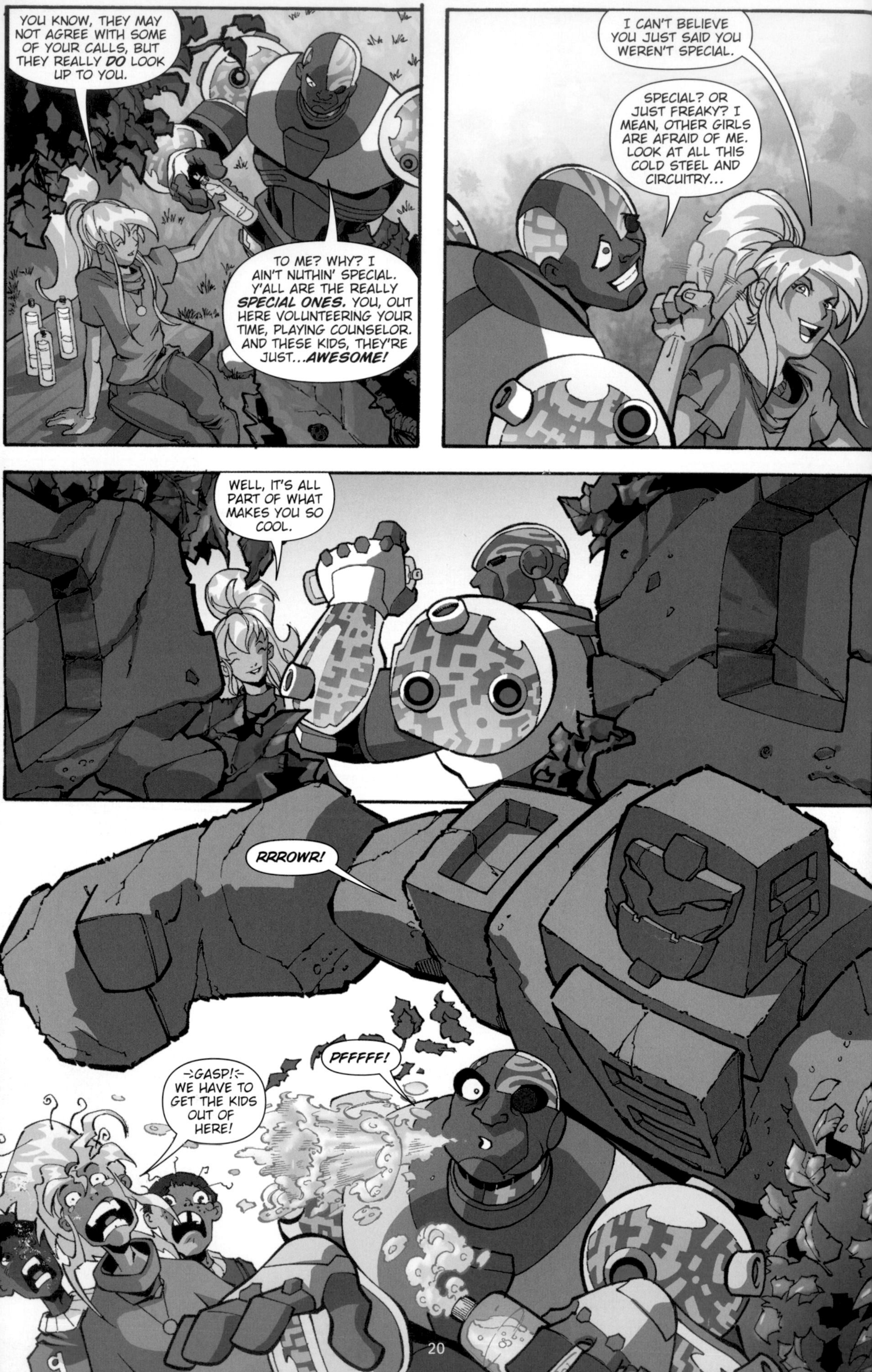
YOU KNOW, THEY MAY NOT AGREE WITH SOME OF YOUR CALLS, BUT THEY REALLY DO LOOK UP TO YOU.
TO ME? WHY? I AIN'T NUTHIN' SPECIAL. Y'ALL ARE THE REALLY SPECIAL ONES. YOU, OUT HERE VOLUNTEERING YOUR TIME, PLAYING COUNSELOR. AND THESE KIDS, THEY'RE JUST...AWESOME!
I CAN'T BELIEVE YOU JUST SAID YOU WEREN'T SPECIAL.
SPECIAL? OR JUST FREAKY? I MEAN, OTHER GIRLS ARE AFRAID OF ME. LOOK AT ALL THIS COLD STEEL AND CIRCUITRY...
WELL, IT'S ALL PART OF WHAT MAKES YOU SO COOL.
RRROWR!
PFFFFF!
-GASP!- WE HAVE TO GET THE KIDS OUT OF HERE!

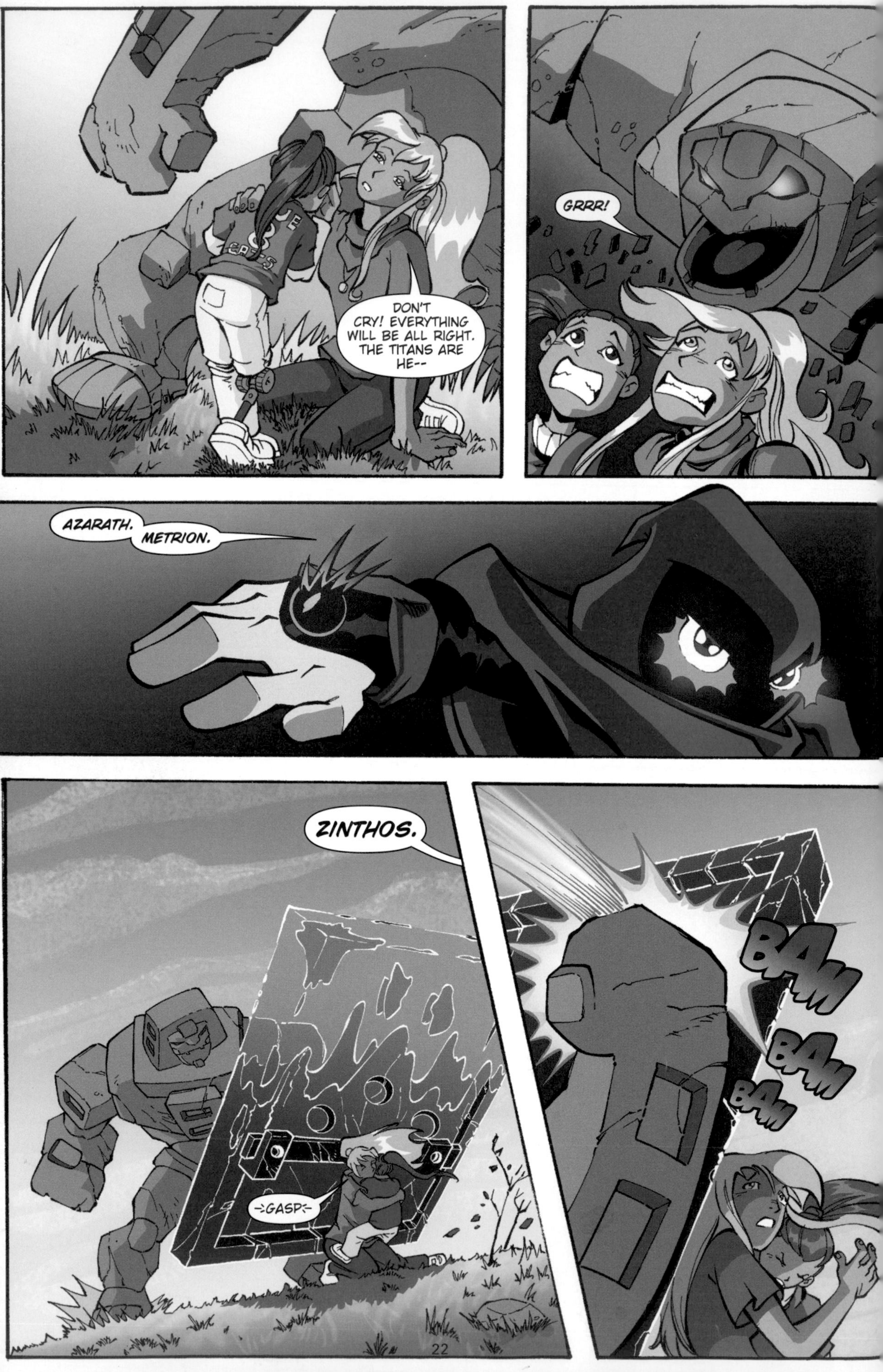
DON'T CRY! EVERYTHING WILL BE ALL RIGHT. THE TITANS ARE HE--
GRRR!
AZARATH.
METRION.
ZINTHOS.
GASP
BAM
BAM
BAM

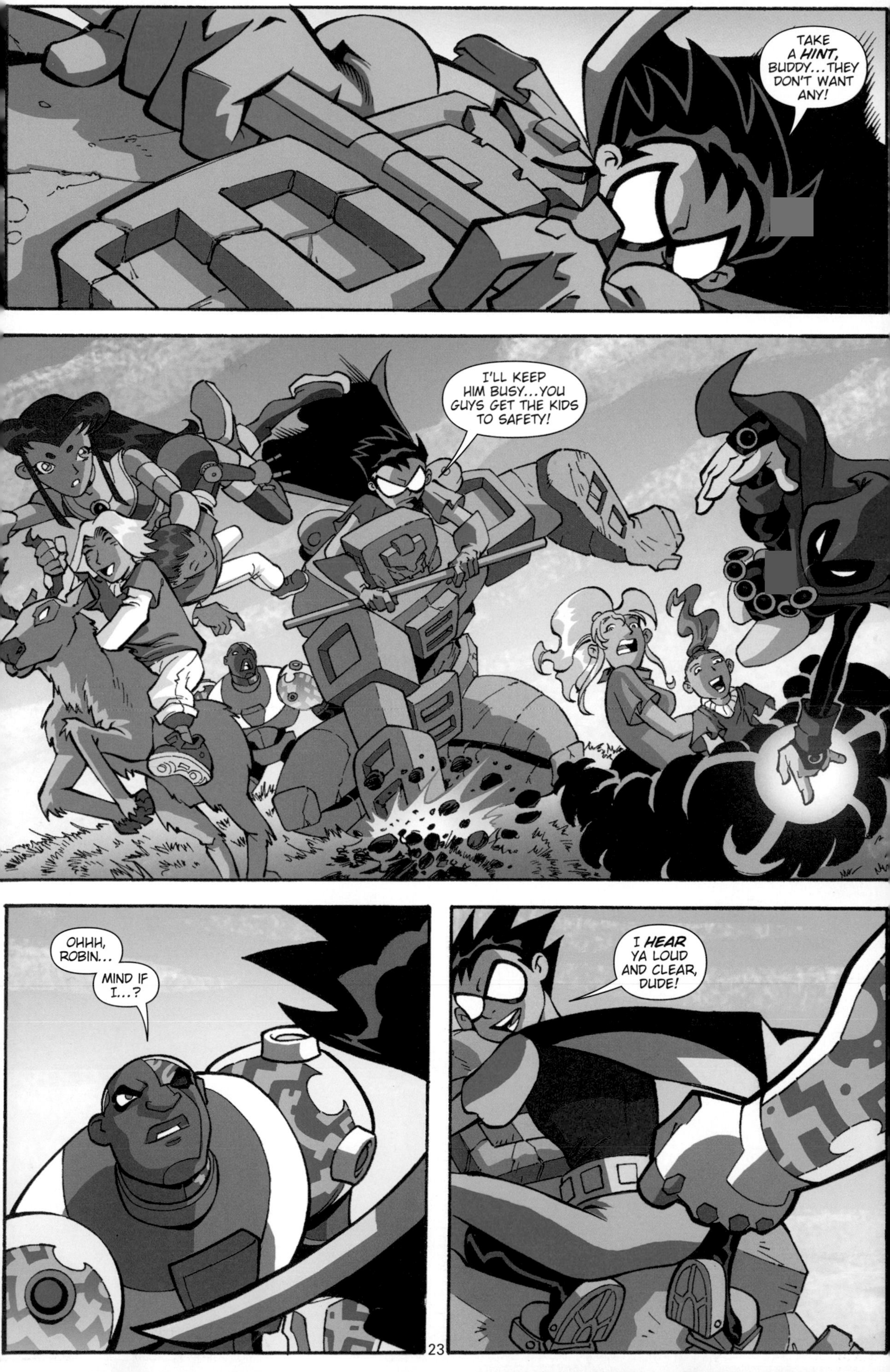
TAKE A *HINT,* BUDDY... THEY DON'T WANT ANY!
I'LL KEEP HIM BUSY... YOU GUYS GET THE KIDS TO SAFETY!
OHHH, ROBIN...
MIND IF I...?
I *HEAR* YA LOUD AND CLEAR, DUDE!

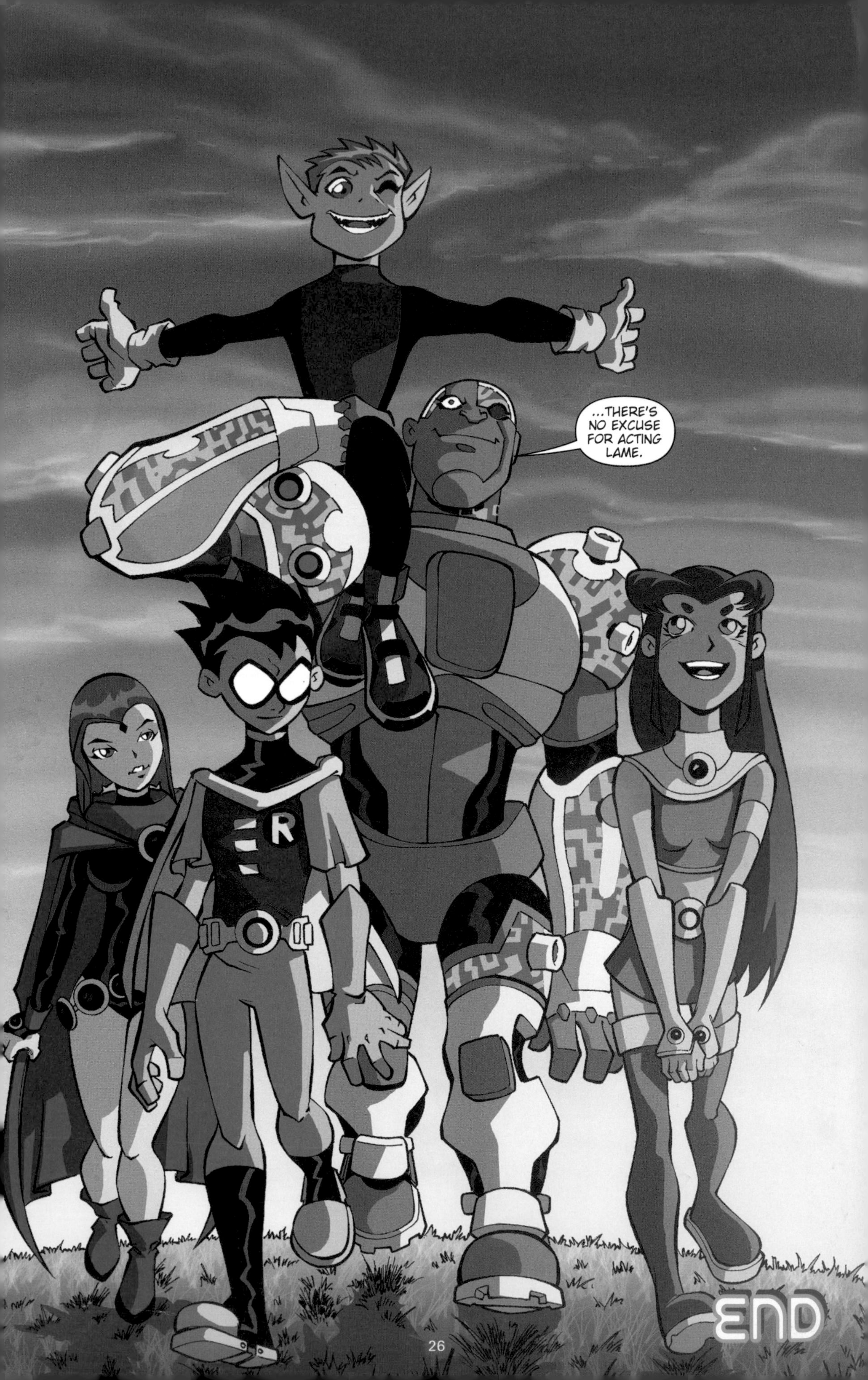
...THERE'S NO EXCUSE FOR ACTING LAME.
END

# CREATORS

## J. TORRES WRITER

J. Torres won the Shuster Award for Outstanding Writer for his work on Batman: Legends of the Dark Knight, Love As a Foreign Language, and Teen Titans Go! He is also the writer of the Eisner Award nominated Alison Dare and the YALSA listed Days Like This and Lola: A Ghost Story. Other comic book credits include Avatar: The Last Airbender, Batman: The Brave and the Bold, Legion of Super-Heroes in the 31st Century, Ninja Scroll, Wonder Girl, Wonder Woman, and WALL-E: Recharge.

## TIM SMITH 3 ARTIST

Tim Smith 3 has done professional work in illustration and design for over eight years. He uses a mix of traditional and computer techniques and has worked for the following publishers: Marvel, DC Comics, Papercutz, Tokyopop, Archie Comics, and a few others.

# GLOSSARY

*adequate* – just enough, or good enough

*assist* – give support or help

*circuitry* – electrical wires and components

*custody* – if someone is taken into custody, he or she is arrested by the police

*destructive* – causing lots of damage

*failed* – did not succeed in a goal or objective

*lame* – weak, unconvincing, or injured

*offended* – irritated, annoyed, or angered by someone's actions or words

*operative* – significant or important

*pleasant* – likeable, friendly, or enjoyable

*withdrawn* – very shy and quiet

# VISUAL QUESTIONS & PROMPTS

**1.** Based on what you know about Beast Boy's character, why is he picking sausage off his pizza?

**2.** Cyborg has a little rain cloud hanging over his head in this panel. Read the surrounding panels on page 12 and explain what he's feeling or thinking.

**3.** The Teen Titans make a great team. Identify three panels in this book where two or more of them work together to get something done.

**4.** Based on his reaction in this panel, how do you think Beast Boy feels about Starfire's comment?

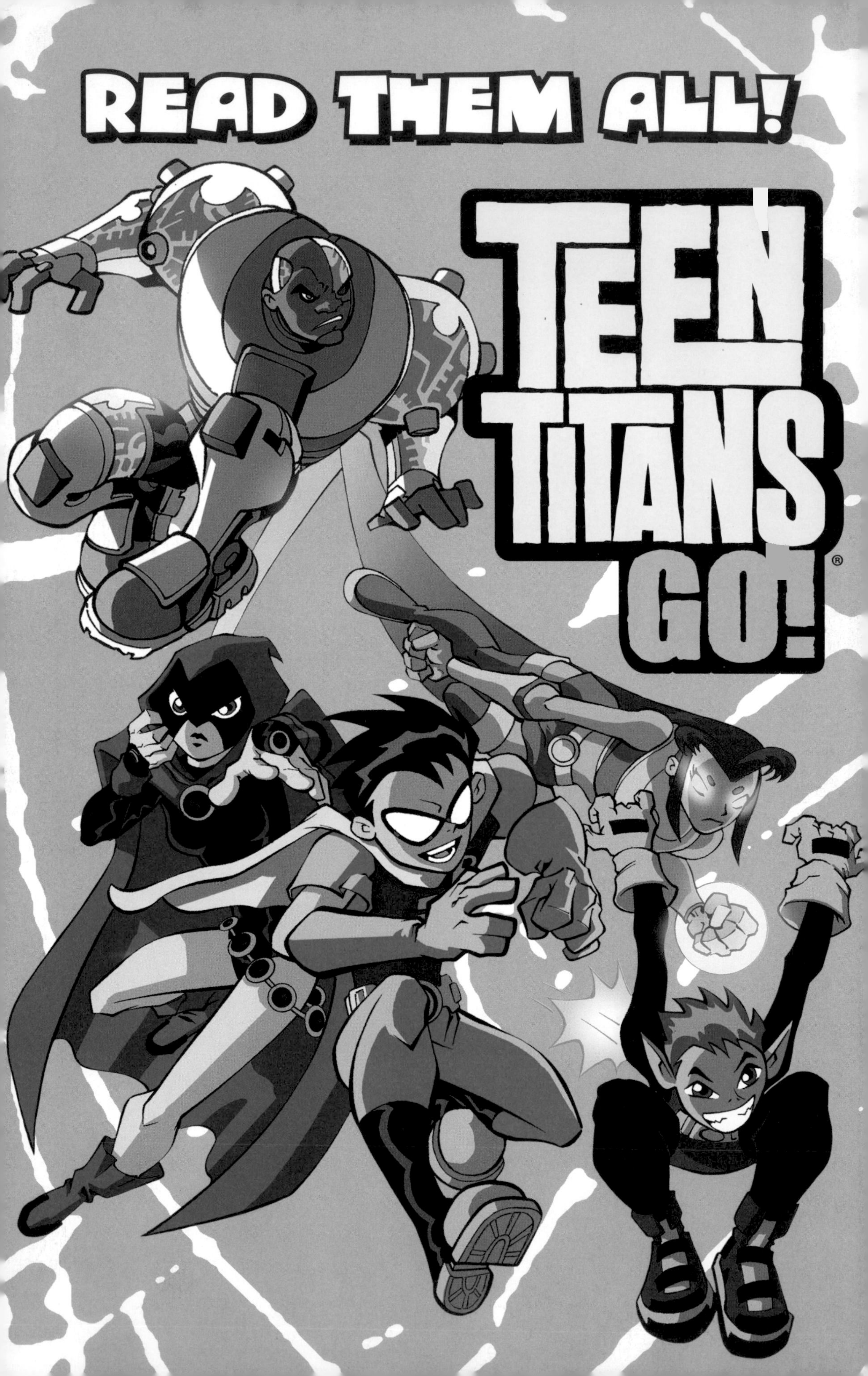
READ THEM ALL!
TEEN TITANS GO!®

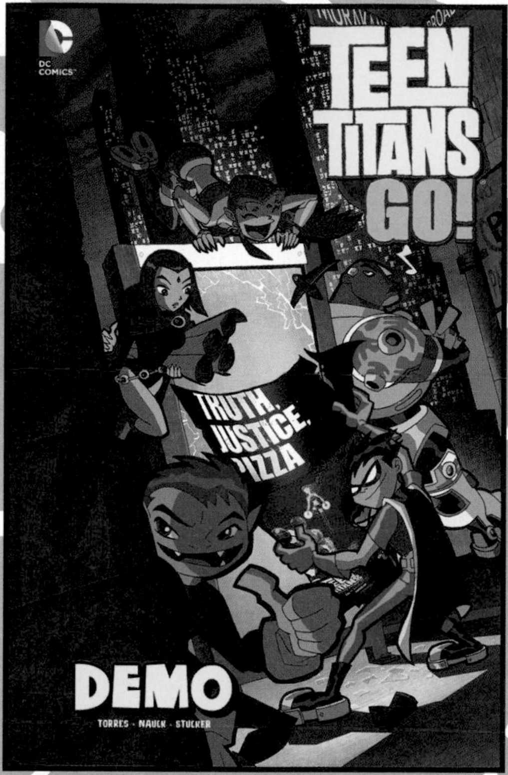
DC COMICS
TEEN TITANS GO!
TRUTH, JUSTICE, PIZZA
DEMO
TORRES · NAUCK · STUCKER

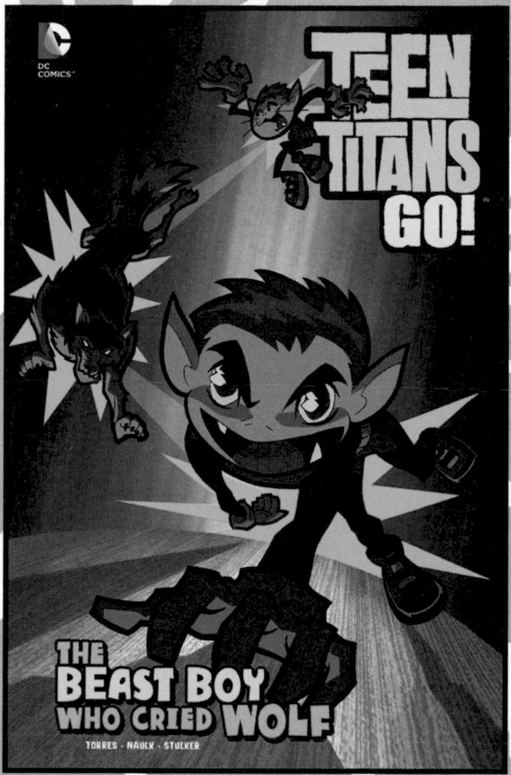
DC COMICS
TEEN TITANS GO!
THE BEAST BOY WHO CRIED WOLF
TORRES · NAUCK · STUCKER

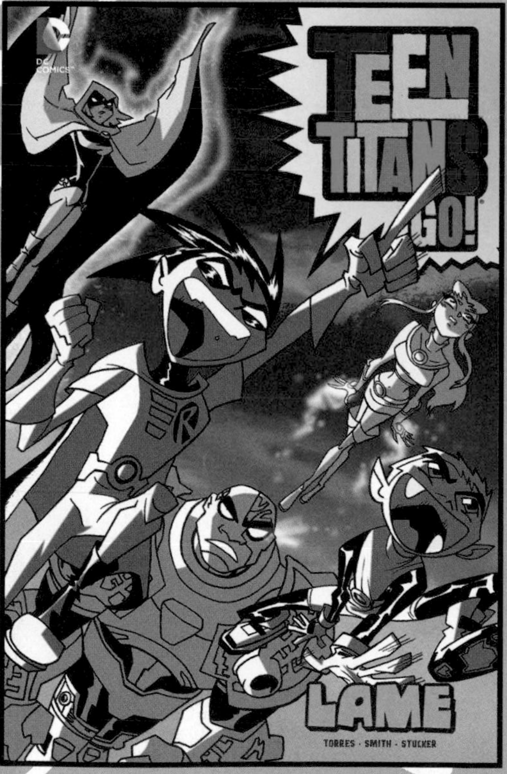
DC COMICS
TEEN TITANS GO!
LAME
TORRES · SMITH · STUCKER

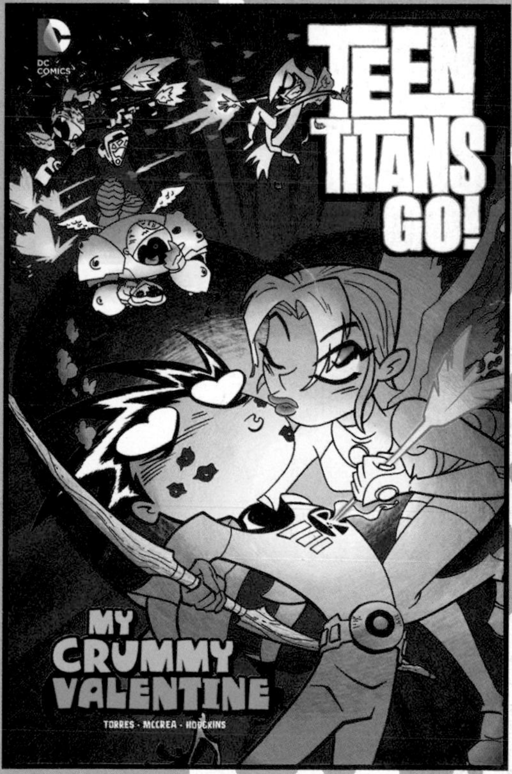
DC COMICS
TEEN TITANS GO!
MY CRUMMY VALENTINE
TORRES · MCCREA · HOPKINS

Raintree

TEEN TITANS GO!®

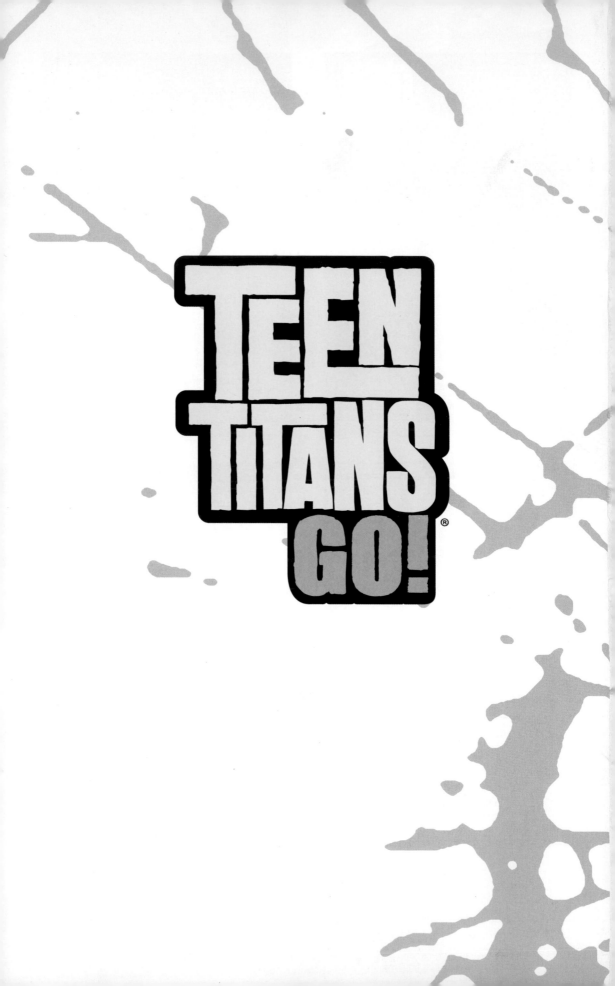